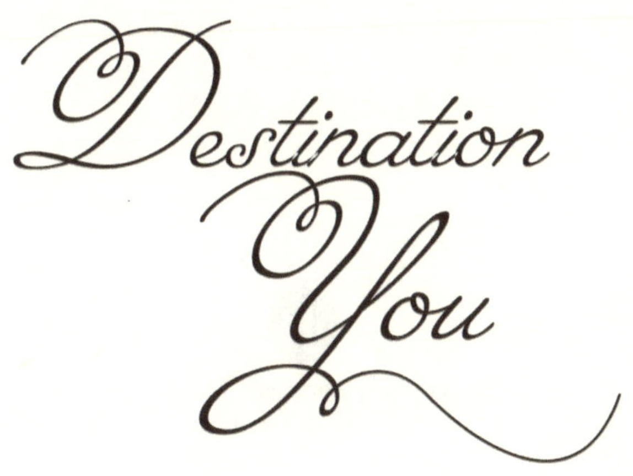

Destination You

KOMALJEET KAUR

notionpress.com

INDIA • SINGAPORE • MALAYSIA

ISBN 979-8-88935-934-0

Life is sometimes relentless, as you are going to fall deep into your journey of thoughts, and it seems inevitable as well. Whether we accept it or not, we have all felt deceived either by our actions or by destiny, which wanted to teach us something. We are all like Panchi, who is an Indian girl living in a world full of hope that, as a cultured daughter, her parents will help her to get what she always wanted: independence, an allowance to study further after graduating from school, on the condition that she would not until then have committed the crime of falling in love, as it will erode the family's pride. In my family, this term refers to male members only, as it does in the majority of small villages, where women have nothing to do with this term. So, life turning upside down can be precisely seen in this story of Panchi when she seems destined to fall in love with someone who has a completely different personality than her.

Chapter One

Panchi

In 2012, Hoshiarpur, one of the oldest districts of Punjab, located in the east of this state, shares boundaries with Jalandhar, Kapurthala, and Gurdaspur. People's lives in this region have always been simple, as anyone can still see traditional Kothis and Havelies built with vernacular and colonial design elements. In the past, there used to be a central courtyard around which all the rooms were built. Even though we were not rich, our great-grandfathers did not leave any stone unturned during the construction of our beloved house. Perhaps they were trying to boast about the money that they gained through extorting government funds that our great-grandfathers received for the good of the town's people. As far as I have heard, they did keep the majority for themselves, and ever since, I have been hearing the true story behind our house. I sometimes wonder: If they had such a big opportunity, why did they miss buying an indiscriminate portion of land that would have been used by us today? Well, it was their wish; it was their rule, and who am I to question their inevitable will? So, it's better if I continue my story.

"Sukhi, turn down the heat," and Sukhi turned it down angrily. Sukhi, by the way, is my uncle's daughter, who was abandoned at the age of 3 or maybe 4 since my aunt was bearing another child who grew up to be a boy, and being an inferior gender, it lowered her importance. My aunt said that she couldn't nurture two children at the same time, so Sukhi's maternal uncles took her away to take care of her. I have been to her maternal house once, and I must admit that was quite an experience as back then both of her uncles were bachelors, and she has an aunt as well who was also not married then; she was given great care by the family, having Nani and Nana as well (her aunt's mom and dad). She was a princess in actuality, being the only child at home, but the case is different now that she is married and her uncles and aunts are married too, having children of their own. During her childhood, she would ask, "What is this house? How are you even managing to live in this? People are kind of a mess here." Me being me, I used to say, "You are not getting the actual picture." But perhaps it was me who was getting the wrong picture.

Chapter Two

Kabil

"Hey! Wait for me, you stop! stop!" screaming and running to hop in the car, Chetan is yelling at me. He knows that I am not going to leave him here while I try to start driving as soon as I can since I do not want to be behind bars. Hey, don't just give me that look; I am a decent guy with a rich family background, but perhaps today was bad. Starting from the beginning, on one Sunday evening in 2013, we were both having a few drinks with some random girls and passing on some adult jokes. Hey, I am a decent guy. You know it's just a tendency of humans to attract the opposite gender, and for that, I was trying my best. My cousin, Chetan, also had similar abilities. So, as I was saying, while passing random jokes and trying to impress the girls, we were so enthusiastic that we forgot the time when we broke a traffic signal one time or maybe two and didn't even stop for the police inquiry; perhaps we underestimated the power of the Haryana police, as I belong to Ambala. So, the worst that could happen was the moment when all our impressing and laughing along with boasting our status finally seemed to convince those girls to exchange phone numbers. "Hey, you!" A person in a police uniform called us, and we were clever enough to understand that it was better to run. Chetan looked at me, and in no time we started running, giving kisses to the girls. I yelled, "Next time, make your phone numbers ready to offer me," and they started laughing.

"It's your fault, you asshole," said Chetan, trying to catch his breath. "Like you didn't do anything." I took a pause and mimicked him, "Asshole," and we started laughing. I started the engine, and he jumped into our Thar 4×4, ours because he is more like a real brother to me, and we have never divided anything, whether it is about the first geometry box that I bought after arguing with my parents or the Chip & Pepper denim that I bought when I was going to turn 16 in June 2006. We have shared clothes, toys, gadgets, or anything that is sort of useful or maybe not, but we never share girls. His girlfriend is my half-sister, and mine is his. I said "half" because maybe someday! who knows! Hahaha. We both have never been in a serious relationship though; we like to keep things simple mostly.

"Shit man! You broke the signal again. This is surely going to take a toll on me." Chetan sounds panicked since the Jeep is running so fast that we have to scream at each other. Driving even faster, I screamed, "And me as well."

"God, I swear I am never going to sit in his car the next time. I would better take an auto rickshaw. God, please save me from this venom," Chetan said sarcastically.

"Ok, so it's me who's bad now." I said surprisingly since the idea was of him remembering the time when he said, "Hey! Don't bother, you. There's no police on the road." What an idiot was he to say so, and what an idiot was I to doubt India's advancement in technology and CCTV?

Chapter Three

Panchi

Looking at the sunset, I am sitting with my four-year-old daughter, thinking about the time my mother made all the promises. "Mom, I am going to be a doctor one day."

"Of course, dear, you can be whatever." My mom replied, assuring me. "Based on one condition only."

I knew what she was trying to say, so to ensure my possibility of getting a higher education, I started making distance from boys in my class when I was nearly 12 years old. Since my aunt told me that "This is your most critical age. Once you get comfortable with them, you want to stay close to them, talk to them, and you may even become a girlfriend, burying family respect with some boy."

Oh my God. Now all that seems completely bullshit not to tell a girl. She should be left free to exploit every man and even woman to explore her wildest side, but when I was in my teenage years, staying away from boys and all the potential girls enjoying themselves with some guys was like God's plan to me.

After making all these sacrifices, what my family had for me was a pick-proof marriage plan right after my 18th birthday. They are all jerks, I tell you. Although they got me married to a good family, my loving husband had the same thought process as them. *I sometimes wonder why, since the very beginning of human civilization being converted into a society, it is only the female sector that needs to remain liable for everything.* Not that male doesn't have a role, he has maybe one or two, earning and abusing, I guess, but a female is always there behind everything to be sacrificed, for leaving her birthplace to adjust to a completely new environment after being married (it is not only she who is getting married but the man as well), bringing someone into the world (yeah, man is important, giving his fucking sperm), nurturing the child, managing the house (and if she is working, managing both), and taking care of everyone's needs (no one doing that in return). God (if there is one) would probably be a man, which is why he is doing all the favors for his side only. I don't know, and I would rather not go into such depth. Well, as I have a four-year-old daughter whom I am completely in love with, I try to spend the time that I barely have after the full day of housework with her. Sometimes my legs and back hurt so much that I don't even want to try taking another step, but it's not up to me whether I want to but on my in-laws. This doesn't bother me at all since I have seen my mother and aunts doing the same and I have always been told to do so. "The less you will make use of your mind, the happier you will keep your family," is exactly what my grandmother once told me. I clearly remember the time when she used to snatch my books and beat me for not working in the kitchen. Her words still hurt like a thorn, which she used to say while commenting on my unfair complexion. "Why are you becoming more of a burden on your father? My son is barely able to run this house, and you want to waste even that much of his income on your studies, too. You should better help your mother with house chores; perhaps then you will somehow be blessed to marry a wealthy man." What is this marriage all the time, and why did I even try to run away from this concept when I knew it was my fate as soon as I turned eligible? My marriage was like, "May you rot in hell."

I hadn't shown a picture of the person with whom I was about to get married and thinking about meeting him was something disastrous. So, there was no chance for me to ask him whether, after marriage, he would let me study. But I convinced him later to try distance learning; that was good; at least I was studying. I got pregnant the same year and had a daughter the next, so somehow God found a way to bless me.

Chapter Four

Kabil

You have to admit that there is something in "Fast and Furious." All you have to do is imagine that Vin Diesel is sitting in the driver's seat and waiting for his buddy, to jump in, just as I was waiting for Chetan. It took us about 20 minutes to reach Mullana from the Pyramid Club, which is in Ambala City. We had to jump off the wall, as ringing the doorbell would not be a good option, so we were trying to sneak in. If I talk about my house, then it is no less than a luxurious palace. It has everything to boast its luxury: an infinity pool, curtains that operate on sunlight, open areas, huge balconies, high-end kitchens, and, of course, security cameras. Because my house is before Chetan's, I told him to stay with me. When we entered, my dear father was waiting for us wearing a kurta-pajama, which is a two-piece garment set and basic clothing for almost all Punjabis. He usually doesn't wear that as he is a professional lawyer, but it is good for comfort, as you know, and those who don't know about this clothing call it a night suit. Punjabis don't generally like that. Stepping away from his wingback chair and folding his arms behind him, he was giving that intense look. Chetan had his mouth filled with water as he directly went to the kitchen to drink water from the fridge, and I was just placing the Jeep's keys down. We were both like we had seen a kind of ghost, two of us staying still, Chetan being the funniest. My dad came closer to me (Chetan moved his eyes toward both of us) and finally said, "I got a call from the police." "It should be the last time, or you will have to forget that you own a Jeep and a Royal Enfield Classic 350." Chetan nearly choked on water and said, surprisingly, "But he doesn't have a Royal Enfield Classic 350."

"Exactly," he replied and smiled, looking at me. We understood why he laughed and we shouted cheerfully while hugging each other. Chetan was still jumping like a kid who just got chocolate candy. I hugged my father and took the keys, but before leaving, he said, "I still mean what I said earlier." We wasted no time and ran out of the door. My father shouted and asked, "Where are you both going at this hour?" "Is this something to ask dad?" I replied. We are ready to unleash the beast, cheering out loud on the streets of Mullana. We may have disturbed a few people's sleep tonight, but who cares when you can vanish within minutes with your new Bullet bike? I have to admit that since I was a child, I have gotten everything that I wanted. I have a younger brother, whom I tease by considering someone adopted, as I am the favorite of everyone in my life: the favorite student with cute dimples for teachers, the favorite boy to date for girls, and the favorite of my loving mom and dad.

I always consider myself lucky, as until now I have never seen hindrances in getting anything except for my studies, you know. I mean, why do you need to study when you are famous among all the female students who are trying their best to not let your parents down with less than a grade B? That's a good thing, right? I get money whenever and wherever I want. My parents generally say, "This is your time, kid. Enjoy! Have fun!" And maybe in a few cases, I have taken that too seriously, looking for better and more persuasive methods to have sexual pleasure with two or three partners sometimes. I mean, why not get everything if you can? It's not wrong to bring happiness to your world on your terms and conditions. Continuing this process, I may have broken the hearts of 3 or 4 beautiful girls, but sometimes they don't understand the ultimate goal of not getting into uneasy relationships but getting the thing that these are made for. By the way, why waste time? That doesn't make sense.

Chapter Five

Panchi

"No, please just don't." Sobbing and requesting sounds I was hearing in my sleep, I thought maybe it was a dream going on, but I woke up into reality after a thud that was not too loud. My father was showing his masculinity over my mother. It was nearly 10:30 at night when I saw him beating and kicking her. He was drunk at the time, and maybe it's due to the after-effects of a drug that heightens our emotions, which he was trying to get on her, and this in no sense is appropriate. I stood up, looking for my mother, hearing her cry. My heart was pounding fast, my hands went cold, and I was nearly dying to know whether she was alright. I was barely standing when I saw her sitting on the bare floor, holding hands as she was trying to protect herself against another slap, but my father stepped back when I called her name out loud. My scream nearly woke up everyone else in the house except the kids, and only my aunt supported her in getting up; others were just looking at the pageant.

"Huff!!" I woke up. Looking at my phone, I remember that was a very old thing.

"What is the matter with you?" My husband was annoyed that I disturbed his sleep.

"I am sorry."

"No, I know you do this intentionally." "Can't you just let me sleep well after working so much?"

I started crying and said, "I am so sorry about that." "I didn't do this to disturb you."

Wearing a sheet, he took a turn and said, "Just shut up!"

Perhaps I cried for what I saw in my dream and not about how rudely my husband reacted, as I have become used to such behavior.

When I was a child, I used to have these dreams less often, but marriage has somehow encouraged this issue of mine. Now, here I am a bit wrong; these are not just dreams but a virtue of the reality of my world and of the lives of thousands of other girls who are being forced to live in circumstances like these.

It's been a while since India has been independent, but is it?

Anyway, it's 4:30, and it's time for me to wake up. Milk is gurgling and is going to be ready for churning; I am kneading the floor. My mother-in-law is going to wake up soon, and so do the other members, such as my husband and father-in-law, but my cute little daughter's time is 7:30 to 8:00. She is old enough for school, but we have put that decision on hold for a few months.

Even though Naraingarh is a small city in Ambala, its calm and serene environment fits my personality well. I just loved being there, and my two favorite places were the State Central Library, as I am fond of reading; you know, it's like looking in the mirror to me; every story tells about a new Panchi. However, we don't live there right now since my husband is in the civil service and has been posted in Chandigarh, so we all had to move here; and the another place was "Devi Lal Herbal Nature Park," which is famous for its medicinal plants. I always wanted to be a doctor, you know, so my interest somehow relates to this field usually. We had to leave such a beautiful area, but we have good neighbors here in Chandigarh. My in-laws don't like me visiting there, but I love cooking, and I love offering something tasty to Saumya. Saumya is a widow living with her mom and two children; Pratik, who is in his 10th grade, has a face that you can't describe in words or phrases, different really and in a quite charming way; he has curly brown hair and a deep set of eyes. He is nearly 5 feet 8 inches tall (a bit taller than me), and very well put together in his body shape (maybe due to the four days a week gym) being nice, especially when it comes to his behavior toward me. He never calls me by my name, nor does he call me by any other reference. It's a kind of time when I get that he is talking to me, as when he says, "Would you pass the remote to me?" and because I am the one near it, I get that he is saying that to me. I think he is a bit shy, but not when he knows I am not around, and the second is Gitika, who is opposite her brother, enthusiastic, witty, and lively type of girl that you can see in any big city, and if I say the opposite, then I mean she is: fair in color but has less attractive facial features; she is short in height (approximately 5.4); that's the reason she usually wears heels and has long, curly hair just like mine. She is one year younger than her brother. She loves talking and making friends, unlike her brother. She has told me thousands of stories about her boyfriends, and a person like her is also on a boyfriend-making spree wheras, the girl who looks nearly half her age, has a 5-year-old daughter. "Shame, baby, what a shame!"

But that's fine, though. Everyone has a different life with different problems, and I am one of them all, dealing with my own.

Saumya's mother, Kaushal, is not like any other lady I have seen in my life but is appreciatively unique. She is supporting her daughter by having her live away from her in laws, allowing her to do something on her own by not depending on others. She is 62 years old and loves it when I pay a visit. I usually visit them between 1 and 2 at noon since I generally complete all the chores by then, and Harsangeet also takes a nap at that time.

Chapter Six

Kabil

Both Chetan and I are free since completing our bachelor's in medicine, as I thought we would better prepare for something to study abroad, but those tests are way out of my league, actually, for both of us. So, instead of wasting two more years after our bachelor's degrees, we have now planned to study further, and for that, what would outcompete the beautiful and most beloved city of Punjabis, Chandigarh? Beautifully located at the foothills of Shivalik, it is one of the best experiments in urban planning and modern architecture of the twentieth century. It is not only known for its well-planned architecture but also for its cleanliness and greenery, and what can one say about the angels living in this city? Damn! I am ready for the thrill, and convincing parents would not be that challenging for such sweet and innocent guys as us. Chetan's dad is a property dealer, and he owns a place or two that would be convenient, but his mother, unlike mine, is a bit humiliating. Whenever he does something, I am the one behind it. He failed the exam "because of the one he hangs out with," as her words go.

He broke his phone. "It's because of Kabil."

He was found with a girl in his bedroom; "he is the one behind it."

Like, really, for every action he takes, which is always wrong, the reason is always me. But he always sings to her mother, "Yeh dosti hum nahi chodenge." Bringing his hand to her, as I have witnessed it once, "Todenge dum magar uska saath na chodenge."

Haha, it's nice to have someone who is always there with you and will always be either good or bad.

"Maybe you are the reason I don't believe in true love," I say to him, and he takes it foolishly. But the true meaning behind this is the fact that love needs to be with someone with whom you can go to your deepest emotions without any shame or overthinking, and I cannot think of any girl who has the patience to listen to my deepest emotions. So, I may consider myself at no fault if someone finds me out toying with random girls' feelings, as the fault is theirs; nearly every girl in my area knows what type of person I am, and if they still choose to be with me, the reason is simple: excitement and pleasure until you get bored. Okay, so before embarking on our idea, we both need to talk to our parents.

Chetan's mother, "But why do you want to go there when there are colleges in Ambala as well, and you studied for your bachelor's here so why not continue for your master's in the same place?"

Convincing though, but I don't judge him on persuasion; he had very good examples to justify his position.

"There are very good colleges in Ambala," he said, slowly mimicking her, "but look at the ones who study here with no opportunities for better career options."

"And what do you have to offer?" "Barely passing with 40% is speaking for career options." His dad said tauntingly.

"And what did you have to offer when we sent you to Delhi for post-graduation?" (Here the battle goes on.) Chetan's grandfather said barbecuing his son.

"Oh, please, dad." Mr. Saini said in defense that "circumstances are different now. Don't you see the news? Youth is spoiled. Addiction is on the rise."

Chetan saw the dice being rolled and did not have another option but to say, "No one loves me here. Everyone is thinking about their own. I know you are afraid of the expenses, but I am not going to ask you for money." Sobbing falsely, "I will work day and night in cafeterias and malls to make my ends meet, and then," encouragingly, "I will get what I want, better career options, and I will never come back to this house." "What I will do here anyway when I would have done everything on my own."

Pointing at his father, he said, "Keep your money; I don't want that."

Well, that was enough. He went to his room smiling, leaving them all shocked and worried.

What a play it was, as he described me. How can they not humor him when, in fact, he is their only child?

My situation, however, is different. I asked my mom, and she was fine. My dad always wanted me to be happy as hell. I remember the time when my school principal called my father once and said, "Your son always causes trouble here in school; that's why I am calling you."

My dad is the king of sarcasm: "He always causes trouble at home." "Did I ever call you?"

The benefits of being a lawyer, I guess, are: never let anyone think you are at fault. Well! We started packing, had fun meeting our families, and said our goodbyes. Goodbyes are not always hard! The only one that is challenging is talking to Tuffy. I hate when someone calls him a dog; he is like a baby to me. Back when I got him, he was a puppy, so he was easier to carry, but now that he is bigger, I sometimes have to pull him forcibly, especially when he gives me that "I don't care" look like he doesn't give a shit about whatever I am telling him to do. I remember when I took him to a nearby park; I swear he was the laziest dog there, and it was hard for me to pull him while he was just sitting on the ground, and I had to give that "that's fun" look to pretty faces walking around. But we used to give each other favors, as when our neighbours moved to Canada and took their pet Gisello far from his boyfriend Tuffy. Tuffy used to be sad for a few days, so I gave him the support that he required, you know, and he is loyal to his words. He generally returned them all by getting something from the kitchen when mom used to not give me dinner because of my low grades, which you can say was stealing. I used to wonder how he managed to reach the kitchen shelf, but now I understand that it was always my mother. *No love can surpass a mother's love. It may sometimes be in disguise, but is always true.* I love them all, standing near the Jeep and watching them wave hands. I may be looking dumb, but deep down I want to make them all proud.

Chapter Seven

Panchi

I heard once that when you love someone, the last thing you want is to lose the chance of seeing them sleep, but whenever my husband comes home late, he wakes me up either because he wants to fulfil his manly desires or because it is about serving him dinner. But I know he loves me since my mother has always told me—*even though he sometimes beats her— my father loves her.* Same as that, my husband loves me even though he doesn't talk to me or doesn't want to listen to me, but who else is he going to love? *The one thing that I am sure about is that pure love is only found between a husband and his wife. There may be a few ups and downs, but the partners always stay together, which is the glory of marriage.* The doorbell rings; it certainly would be my husband. It is 10:30, and everyone else is sleeping. I am wearing loose pajamas and a t-shirt twice the size of mine; it was late, and my husband's clothes are very comfortable. I am near the door in the kitchen, standing and waiting for him to come, so I would serve him since I don't want him to come in the room ordering me loudly and disturbing Harsangeet's sleep, but it was Sanket, my husband's co-worker.

"Hi Bhabhi," he greeted me upon entering, and I smiled and shook my head.

"Arnav is going to be late today due to an urgent meeting with the governor the day after. So, he will be late preparing for that."

"But he didn't say anything about it," I said in wonder.

"Yeah! must have been skipped from his mind. Working man, you know, but how do you know what that means?" He replied tauntingly and supported my husband's side. I was not sure whether I should invite him home at this hour, but I did it anyway.

"Ok, come inside, please." "The food is almost ready."

"I would love to at such a time when you are alone without your husband, but I can't today." "Next time when you are alone, just let me know."

There was a two-second pause. "For dinner." He said it smilingly.

He was standing for my response, but I shut the door in his face. Did I do the right thing? He is my husband's best friend anyway. I don't know. As he is not coming tonight, I put the things in their places. My life is nothing exciting, but being in this house, I tend to enjoy playing with my little daughter and, secondly, nurturing the fish that we have. It was typically my sister-in-law's idea to keep two aquariums. She also has a daughter and is planning for another child (that needs to be a boy only). I love when they eat their favorite Salt and Pepper Corydoras and sometimes Ember Tetra. As I have only fed them these, I have started considering these two of their favorites. There are typical oscillations in their bodies that make certain sounds, and I don't know how this beautiful creature with such a beautiful sound can make me fall in love with it. My mind just soothes down when I sit around the bowl, and these are like two little Harsangeets to me—cute and developing babies.

Here's the next day. Rise and shine I am saying to myself, kissing my daughter's face, I looked at her for a few minutes and finally woke up. It's 4:30 and my husband is still not home, but I love it when he is not around—a bit of relief from something that I don't know. I am coming down the stairs, watching the photographs along the wall. Our house is not very big, but it is nice. We live in Mohali, also known as Shahibzada Ajit Singh Nagar, which is most famous for its grand stadium, the IS Bindra Stadium, or commonly known as Mohali Stadium. Although there is a lot to do in such a big city, I like to stay home. I was cherishing the memories when the doorbell rang. Thankfully, I was awake, and I was wearing a salwar suit that I generally wear, and when I opened the door, it was (unexpectedly) my husband. I greeted him cheerfully, but he didn't respond well. Giving his bag to me, he passed down the hall, where he sat on the couch. I rushed to grab a glass of water for him, and when I came back, he said, "Please take off my shoe, darling."

I hesitatingly asked, "What you just…?"

He held my arm and pulled me down, saying, "Do it already."

What could I say? "He is not beating me as my father; he is just asking me to take his shoes off." I was repeating it in my mind, doing what he said. *The world has to change its way of characterizing domestic violence. I think when you are being tortured, not only must it be a physical beating but also abuse; the punishment for both should be equal.* Everyone has his way to stay calm when he is put into places like these, so I have my own, comparing myself with my mother and concluding that I am way better than her when it comes to the quality of life.

Well, after this chaotic situation, finally it's the time when I can visit Saumya's. Although she is a widow, her father left her mother a fortune and good luck, so it's easier for her mother to support her by bringing up two kids together, plus Saumya's husband was in the army, and due to this, she got a government stipend. Lucky her, I guess, for staying without a husband with your kids and getting everything done even without doing anything to earn a living. When you enter her house, you see a bougainvillea hanging down the wall, and then you go through the garden with mesmerizing plants such as roses, hibiscus, and plumeria. Sometimes when I come here, I see Pratik changing the soil and watering the plants. I love when someone takes care of species other than their own. Today as well, I am walking down the pathway; he is kneeling and sweating, but unlike his usual attire, he is wearing a light-colored T-shirt and shorts along with a moisture-wicking workout sweatband. Any 16-year-old me would have fallen for him. I told you that he sees me only when I am not looking at him; once I caught him though, when her mother wore me a saree and left a drape opened, and Pratik entered without knocking. They had both just come from school, and he was drinking water from his bottle by the time he opened the door. He stood there looking at me for nearly a complete minute, slowly gulping down the water. There was an intense look in both our eyes. I got red and cold, having a half-covered belly, when Saumya said, "Hey! Did you forget to knock?" which broke something that was going on between us, even though it was only for half a minute. Her sister then entered, "Oo la." It's our Panchi. Didi, you need to come to my school someday, and with this saree, you are going to make every single boy go mad out there." Harsangeet laughed, which made me smile. I have to admit, though, that it felt good to see myself in some different attire than my usual salwar suit.

Chapter Eight

Kabil

"Wow! What a beautiful city." Chetan said this in excitement as I was driving us to Chandigarh. It is not that we had come here for the first time, but this time we had come to live here. "We should first have a look at the place that we are going to settle in." I offered.

"Oh! Don't you worry? I trust my dad. He is not going to let us live in the dump. I don't trust my mom though."

We both laughed at it when I took a turn to Zirakpur, where we bought a fully furnished 5-BHK independent house facing other houses with almost similar designs. The fun fact is that the people living next door were Aroras; we got that from the nameplate. Punjabis don't usually get along with them, you know. While we are taking our stuff up the house, a fine-looking girl shows up—every girl is fine-looking to me—and says, "Hi, I am Kiran." Pointing in the other direction, she said, "That is our house, and I am living with my grandparents here." Chetan from behind me goes, "And I am Chetan, but those who love me call me Moon.

What a coincidence that we got it. Kiran and the Moon." Laughing alone.

Kiran pointed at me and said, "You are new here." Tell me if you need anything. Chetan can in no way bear to leave a chance. "Yes, we sure will, Kiran."

But she is still looking at me, so I guess she will not leave until I say something like, "Thanks, but I guess we can manage."

"Are you out of your fucking mind?" Chetan elbowed and asked, surprisingly. "What a beautiful girl she is, and what luck have you got that all of these ask for you always. But you are not giving a shit."

"She is not even that beautiful."

Chetan is right, though, and I have never let a chance go by without getting hooked up. I don't understand— maybe because she didn't look that attractive. I think I fell for some girl once. Back in high school, I had a pretty nice girlfriend, but she dumped me for some nerd so she could use him for her assignments. What a clever bitch she was. So, that was enough experience for me to understand that no girl on this planet is going to stay with you it with unless you have something to offer. In my world, I give girls free will to either continue the process or leave; it's completely on them since there is only one rule: pleasure with no strings attached. No offense, but life should always be that easy.

Well! We have unpacked almost everything, and about the remaining stuff, we will see that tomorrow. Neither of us knows how to cook, so it's better to eat something out. We headed to Barbeque Nation in Sector 26, and while we were there, "Look at those beautiful girls." Chetan said.

I looked at them and replied, "Yeah!" "Fine are these?"

One of them is wearing a tight tank top with a skirt, and the other a loose boyfriend t-shirt with denim. Both of them have sneakers on, and then my eyes are stuck on a girl walking down the other table. "Are these appearing to you in slow motion?"

Chetan answered, giving an awkward look, "No." "But why are you asking?"

"Because she is appearing differently as someone from another planet."

Now we are both looking at her, wide black eyes, a small nose, and round lips. When she is closer, it is easier to see her hourglass body shape, even though she is wearing a suit. She has a fine skin complexion, is not too fair, and has long hair tied with a height of nearly 5.7 inches.

I have never observed any girl in such detail. She is not looking at anyone; it says that she is shy and has come with a little girl, a lady looking double her age, and another girl, who must be in her teenage years.

The waiter is standing near me, and Chetan is saying something that is nearly meaningless. Everything seems meaningless right now as all the other living beings have gone out of existence, blurred out.

"Kabil!" Chetan yelled my name.

"Yes yes! what happened?" I am asking as have recently woken up from a dream. He is asking my opinion on ordering something. But it still took me some time to adapt back to reality. Even after placing an order, I am still trying to have a glance at her. It's like a child of the 90s looking at her favorite female actress in actuality. That would appear funny, but to me, she is representing Madhubala. "Whaaaaat! Don't you dare tell someone this cheesy line that you are thinking about?" I was telling myself, "Have I gone mad? Why am I talking to myself? Stay calm." "What is wrong with you, man?" Chetan asked in surprise. "Why are you acting so strange?"

What can I tell the guy who always asks the reason for not appreciating a girl? Now, this is me. I am acting weird just with the presence of this girl, and now that we've met our eyes for a complete period of eleven seconds, what on earth can throw me back to life?

Chapter Nine

Panchi

It's May 11 and Gitika's birthday. Unlike others, this family usually celebrates birthdays with some of their closest friends. Saumya invited me and Harsangeet to have dinner with them, but not at home. She was talking about some Barbeque nation, which, considering the traffic in Chandigarh, would probably take half an hour to reach. Talking about the scenario when she called on the phone. My mother-in-law picked it up and said, "Hello! Oh, Saumya." Then she gave me a look. I don't remember if I have talked about this, but they both don't like each other. This was back when Saumya was wearing shorts and entered our house.

"O, my god! Where the culture of Indian women has gone. When I was a girl, I barely ever took off my veil over my head; look at the girls today. They have no shame."

That was a straight taunt, but Saumya is not the one who would stand quiet after such a comment.

"And making your daughter-in-law a full-time worker without letting her live as per her wish is what your culture teaches." Shit!

Then she added more: "Relax! Don't give her that look; she has never told me or anyone else about this. People like us can easily learn about people like you. Understanding between two generations, you know." That was direct. Bravo! I am proud of you, my dear friend. She wants me to inhibit all these qualities, but Panchi is Panchi; she is unique in her way. I take it as a compliment to myself, you know. *It's good to have an excuse for not doing what you should be doing.* Alright, so we're heading back to where we were. "Yeah, she is here." My mother-in-law told her, and I knew for sure she was asking for me. Then she told me about the plan, and I had 1 hour for preparing dinner so I can go with her, but I didn't tell anyone that we are going outside; it is just an Indian thing, bearing the courage to ask for what you can never imagine being granted.

So, with Harsangeet, I went to Saumya. When I reached her, she was probably waiting for me. "Here you have come. The girl, holding love for everyone." Saumya said sarcastically.

"Oh, stop it," I replied. "Everyone is holding onto love for someone. I am not alone in that. Most of all, you, with whom I can spend as much time as I want, are still less for her." Saumya is getting closer. "You don't know, but there is something in you, my birdie, that can attract almost everyone. I always love you like my half sister," she said so and kissed me on my cheeks. I am very shy, so I kind of blushed at that. Then the sound comes: "The wait is over." "Behold your heart so that it can bear the pressure of witnessing beauty in a mere human body."

"And what is that?" I asked.

"Angel, Panchi di." "I am an angel who has come to this planet in human form."

We all laughed that even Harsangeet got the actual satire, which made it even more amusing.

Then we headed to the restaurant. Saumya told me in the way that Pratik had taken her grandmother to some physiotherapy sessions. He is quite an obedient son. "I sometimes imagine his life, like what he would do when he gets older. It's not that I am concerned about his job or anything, but it's more about finding connections, you know. He is very quiet and calm. How would he handle a heartbreak?" his mother said while driving. "Oh, my mother, it's okay if he falls in love with someone first." Gitika offered.

"Yeah, she is right." "These things find their ways." I added making her understand to not carry such a burden and she nods. Now that we have reached the place I am headed to carry Harsangeet from the backseat, and Gitika is looking at the mirror, assuring her makeup.

I don't get how she manages to walk in such a short and tight dress. I would have fallen one or two times, but wearing it first is a dream come true. My clothes usually cover every inch of my skin, leaving only my feet, a small portion of my arms, neck, and face, of course. Maybe it's because I don't like being noticed, or there would be some other reason that I still haven't thought of. Well! As we enter through an eye-catching entrance, soothing music is playing. The environment is very calm, having green features added to its interior. I loved the wise colors they painted and the eye-comforting lights. Harsangeet is very excited, and so am I. Our table is in the right-hand corner, facing an aquarium. It's like the owner knows exactly what I want in a place like this. We have ordered vegetable rice with naan bread. They both want me to try Italian, so we have also ordered lasagna and cannelloni. "Kabil," I heard a voice. Two boys are sitting opposite our table. I don't know what happens there, but all I can see is a boy looking straight at me where our eyes meet. Now, this is going to make it difficult to sit. One thing that I wanna make clear is that I don't like being noticed, and when a boy like him who is pretty charming, not to mention, looking at me nearly without blinking his eyes even for a moment, it's hard to admit that I am comfortable.

"Mom, I want to pee." Great. Now I have to walk down the restrooms, crossing his table.

"Ok! But can you hold on for some time? We will be home soon." I am like a mad person asking my 4-year-old child to hold on to her urine. Wow.

"What is it?" Saumya asked.

"It's Harsangeet. Asking to pee."

"Oh! "That is down the hallway." She said.

"Thanks." even though I know it.

So, now I am standing up and passing him, trying not to black out and fall into his arms. "Why is he not looking at someone else?" I am asking myself this as there are so many pretty girls around here in jeans and short dresses. Harsangeet is holding my finger, and when we are coming back, I see someone familiar, and it's Sanket with his two more friends.

"Hey Bhabhi". Great. What else is left as a blessing, my dear God?

"Hello," I replied, and I made my way down.

"What's so in a hurry? Won't you ask your beloved brother-in-law how he is doing?"

I forced a smile to turn to him and say, "I am sorry, but I am with a friend. So, some other day perhaps."

"Look, you didn't call me today as well. I told you to do so when your husband is not around." They all laughed out loud, which is making the conversation a bit more uncomfortable for me to be a part of.

"Is there a problem?" The person who was sitting opposite us asked. How come he is here though?

Sanket replied, "I am talking to my loving Bhabhi, and who are you, by the way? It's none of your business."

But the boy is still looking at me. He comes closer and asks me, "Is everything alright?" The assuring look and the calm sound that he has I don't remember a time when someone talked to me with such deep concern, and we don't even know each other. I didn't say a word, and we are both looking at each other. He has to look a little lower due to the difference in our heights.

"Come, Bhabhi, you should not be talking to a stranger," Sanket said, holding my arm fiercely.

I straightened my arm with one fell swoop since his touch scared me.

The boy angrily grabbed his collar and wall-mounted him, saying, "No asshole has the right to touch a girl without her consent." "Do you get it?"

He was choking, and to a great surprise, none of his friends helped rescue him. I tried to make him let him go by holding the boy's arm, and he did exactly what I wanted him to do. He left him with just the touch of my hand, which was extremely surprising. How can a person's emotions be changed so soon? We are both standing and looking at each other when he sees my daughter cuddling up to my legs.

Chapter Ten

Kabil

"Are you out of your dear mind? What was that? It hasn't even been a day since we came here, and you have already started showing your power." Chetan is yelling at me.

"Oh shut up! It's not even that big a deal. I did what I felt was right."

Chetan turned to me and continued, "Did the girl ask for your help? No, right? Then why did you need to be a hero?" There is silence between us now as he is driving us both back home. How can it be that in this city where there is so much noise, I can't help but listen to the story of that girl's silence? Now that we are back again, what I see through my window is a girl. Looking a little closer, she is no one else but Kiran, who offered us help when we were here in the evening. She is trying to seduce me, which I am sure of as she knows that I can clearly see her through my window. What I did later is wrong in a man's way. I shut my window with a sound and veiled it fiercely. Now, I know that something is definitely wrong with me. As soon as I laid on the bed,

I started thinking about that girl again. What was it like in those eyes that I kept staring at them? What was there on those lips that told me thousands of things without saying anything? Is there anyone else who has thought about someone like this? There was something in her.

"Let's get up now." Who else is it going to be but Chetan?

"It's 10:15, and we were supposed to reach it at 9:45."

He is probably talking about college.

"Wake up, fella; you will get insulted on the first day itself, and you will drown me too."

He is absolutely talking about college.

"Hey." He shouted angrily.

"Yeah, yeah, I am up. I am up. Where's my morning coffee?"

"Shanta Bai, present the favorite coffee you have prepared for your capable sir. Oh sorry for your Kabil, sir." He said it jokingly.

"Asshole." I blurted it out.

He looked at me and then again said, "Get ready."

"I heard that once, Shanta Bai. I am going to take a shower; make that coffee."

"I am not your father's servant. You moron." Chetan is saying so, but I know my friend.

When I came back, I saw there was coffee on the table.

"I love you so much, Shanta." And then I kissed him on his cheek.

He said, rubbing his palm on his cheek, "This much is not enough."

"Let me kiss you on your lips, darling."

He is screaming and pushing me away, "People of the world, save me from this oppressor."

We both are screaming as we pass through the corridor, where we see a couple of old women looking as if they have been taken aback by seeing the ruining culture of India.

So, here we are at the college. Being late is definitely a concern, but who cares about missing a lecture or two when you are here in Chandigarh seeing different people from a unique and colorful world? What a great feeling we are both getting while passing down the hallway looking for the class. When we have reached there, we see that everyone is sitting quietly and listening to the lecture very carefully as per the demand of the subject, constitutional law. I know that's a bit different from my previous educational degrees, but I think I am good at negotiating, maybe inhibiting the quality of my father.

So, why not try your luck in something new, and as for Chetan, he is my soulmate, so he can never think of abandoning me anyhow or anywhere.

"So save these maharathis of ours who have been late by two hours on the very first day of class." As we enter, the professor tries to make us pay for what we have done by being late, which makes everyone else laugh.

"Don't doubt our ability to be good students just because we are late." How do I skip a turn?

Everyone is laughing along with all the pretty girls.

"What is your name?" The professor asks.

"Kabil. That's why I told you about my potential. My name stands for itself." As I am walking down the aisle and looking at the pretty faces, some have eyes on me and some on both of us. Now, that's what I call fun. After the lecture, a girl comes and says, shaking hands, "Hi, I am Diksha." "I get that you are new here."

"Tell me if you need anything." I guessed in my mind.

Which is what she exactly said? "Tell me if you need anything," by writing down her phone number on my palm. "I heard you've got the potential. So, let's check how much." That is a good and seductive move, I have to admit.

She moves out, giving me that look that is like an open offer to something that I don't think I am going to let go of. Although Diksha is pretty impressive, sorry babe you are late. Someone else has made me lucky. I said to myself thinking about that girl.

Chapter Eleven

Panchi

"Oh! Look, madam has come too. So soon?" My husband is leaning forward as I am settling Harsangeet on the bed. "Did you forget that you have a house and a husband, and you have some responsibilities for that?"

"Haan?" His voice goes louder this time.

"Shall we chat outside?" I asked him, looking at my sleeping daughter. There is a thing to consider: my daughter is only my daughter and not his.

"The pot is called the kettle black. You are not the place to make deals. Where have you been the whole time?" He asked.

I took a step back, wiping my mouth because I needed water. "We were at Saumya's. I told you about her daughter's birthday." He angrily pulled me towards him: "Then why were you at Barbeque Nation? Haan! Tell me."

Now what do I have to say? "She changed the plans. I am sorry. I should have asked you first."

"Yeah, you should, but you didn't." I thought the conversation was going to be finished here, but he proved me wrong. His one hand was enough to make me realise my mistake. As I was on the floor, the time flew before my eyes when I was in school. "Do you know that remembering God too much can change our luck?" One of my friends told me.

"Really," I said, extremely hopefully. I knew about my luck from the beginning and knew that I had to change it. From then on, I woke up early every day to visit Gurudwara Sahib. Every day was an act of service. I never let go of any opportunity where I could come before the eyes of God. But perhaps God knew that I was doing all this for my own selfishness and to demand something from Him in return. That is why he has doubled my every punishment since then, and this slap was to remind me of my status as well as that I have done something wrong, which was the unique feeling I was having for the stranger. Under no circumstances should a married woman feel anything about anyone other than her husband. I was almost lying on the ground with disheveled hair, fear, and remorse in my eyes when my husband explained the exact reason for his act of anger.

"How long has this been going on?" He bowed down and asked me.

"What do you mean by what's going on?"

"You and Sanket."

"What?" I didn't seem to understand as everything seemed to have stopped. Everything was lying as if water had stopped quenching thirst and the sun was raining cold instead of sunshine. Is it justified to think that way?

"You are doubting me?"

"How can I not?" Sanket has told me everything. You kept on putting strings on him, knowing that he is such a good friend of mine. Punching the wall hard, he said, "That's why you went to that hotel because Sanket was also going to go there." This time, as he was moving toward me with more anger and kicking my stomach, he said, "Why don't you die instead of being such a wife?" I didn't say anything to my husband in defense of this, and I wasn't crying this time. *I was just missing and trying to understand my mother, who used to try to put herself in a compartment all her life where there was neither light nor her voice heard. Maybe she is still doing the same. Looking at the stars, I want to hear the answer from the universe about whether locking ourselves in a box is a solution.*

My husband didn't sleep in our room, but instead the couch in the living room was more comforting to him. The next morning, I started doing my job as a good wife again. I made tea for everyone and gave it to my husband too, but he left without eating anything. I was feeling bad for him despite the fact that my stomach was still hurting and there was a change in my gait. No one in the house even bothered to ask what happened to me, as the slap mark was still visible on my cheeks. To my surprise, this is nothing new. I think I should better isolate myself for a few days. Harsangeet tries to please me for taking her out for an evening walk, but my mother-in-law is thankfully helpful in this way. It's been 3 days since that, and the scar on my cheek is still very visible. I am not thinking of moving out of my house until it is gone. But then I heard a very loud knock at the door. On opening it, I see that Gitika is panting very loudly. "Granny wants to see you." "Something is not right with them, come quickly with me." After hearing this, I did not stay for a minute and left with her, forgetting what they would say to me when they saw my scar.

"Where's Granny?" I am asking Saumya as she is in such shock after looking at me.

"What happened to you?" "Are you alright?" She was concerned.

After she removed her hand from my cheek, I said that I was fine. "Nothing is wrong with me. Why are you not answering me? Where is Granny?"

"She is absolutely fine and is sleeping right now. What Gitika told you earlier was a lie. I called you on the phone yesterday, and your mother-in-law picked up and said, You have gone to your parents. But we see Harsangeet with her every evening. So, as we all know, something is not right with you. I am sorry that we had to lie to you, but there wasn't any other option."

I took a deep breath and told her to assure her that I was absolutely fine. "Oh really, then what do you have to say about the mark on your left cheek?" I was thinking about something, and then Pratik continued, "We know that this is your life, but it does not mean that you should make any excuse to cover this act of your husband, so we believe that." He left me in surprise, as I have told you before that Pratik doesn't really talk much, and when it is about me, he usually finds it better to change his plans than coincidentally meeting me. But here he is, standing, looking at me in deep concern. I sat on the couch and started crying, holding myself in both my hands. "It's ok, Panchi di, we are always with you." "You can count on us no matter what it is about." Gitika kneeled down and said to me.

This is all actually relaxing and making me realise that it is not necessary that only those relations with whom we are related by blood are true and the rest are nothing but mere pretense. And in my case, blood relations have never proved to be wise.

"We are gonna find a solution. Trust me." Saumya is showing me hope for something good. It's been two days since I went to Saumya's house. My husband is about to come home, so I have heated dinner for him.

When he came inside, I caught his bag from his hands and started taking off his shoes as soon as he sat on the couch. It looks like he wants to tell me something.

"Come here and sit with me." He pointed to his side. "I'm sorry for what happened that day; I shouldn't have taken a decision just by listening to Sanket." He is sitting there gazing at me, waiting to hear something very enthusiastic as if I will hug him and open my mouth to say that I have forgotten that long ago. But this never happens. Every single day, when I am reminded of what I am capable of and what I am not, I have placed an intoxicated watchman in my heart and mind who does not allow anyone's sympathy to reach my soul. Now, it's just the body that reacts, and what it reacts to is not natural but a mere mask to pretend. "It's ok. That was just a misunderstanding." As I said, he makes a happy face. "Ok, so from now on, we are going to live as a happy couple, and I am going to make everything come true to please you." "What do you want?"

I am just looking at him. "Just tell me." At this time, my heart is crying out loud; I want to go away from you and this show of your false love. But instead, "I want to do something. Maybe a job. Now that I have a degree, I think I can get employed as a teacher." I am just watching his logic and waiting for that one Yes from his mouth.

Chapter Twelve

Kabil

"Where did you die?" "Come on now." I am waiting for Chetan to come, calling him on his phone.

"I'm right behind you; wait a minute."

Then I saw that girl. Yes, the same girl is leaving right in front of my eyes. "She is going, Chetan, she is going." I am yelling at him.

"Now which girl?" He asked in a confused state.

"My dream girl bastard."

It looks like I am standing at the station at around 11 a.m. and my last train is leaving.

Even before Chetan sat down, I was driving so fast that the whole college would be hearing the screeching of tires. Now she has turned and is standing along the wall of the parking lot. Am I going to drive through the middle of it?

Chetan shouts from behind, "She is not even that far. Slow down." I stopped the car just near her. Don't know how it stopped, but by the grace of God. There is no doubt that I have scared her because she is covering her eyes with both hands and she is still stiff even after the car has stopped. I jumped over the open hatch of the car and sat on the bonnet. After slowly taking her hands off her face, I whispered, "Are you alright?" I yearned to hear her voice; I yearned to have a glimpse of her, but she is saying nothing but just looking at me. *The distance between us is nearly zero. Nevertheless, why does she seem so far away?*

"Are you mad? Can't you see?" A woman who was with her that day too is coming towards me, shouting angrily, but I am still yearning to hear something from her mouth alone. "Panchi, are you alright?" She asked and looked at her.

I am still on the bonnet. "Panchi. Panchi is your name?" I asked her in a low voice, and she was nodding her head in slow motion. My car is going backwards, but we are only looking at each other. Everything else is as if it did not exist. Oh, wait, I saw her going and shouted from behind, but she didn't stop nor did she slow down. But this time I will not let her go without talking to me. So because of this, I blocked her way. Whichever side she wants to go to, I am not letting her go. It is not right, but this time everything is right. "What do you want? Should I talk to the principal of your college?" The lady goes again.

"With due respect, I don't want to hear from you." I told her with folded hands.

I said to the girl, "How are you here?" "Have you come to take admission?"

I am eagerly waiting for a "yes" from her.

But instead, "I have a child, and I am married." I am like, "What difference does it make?"

She is staring at me, and I don't know, but now it doesn't matter even if I get slapped by the woman with her. What should I say? How is her voice? I guess it's more than just soothing. The word hasn't come into existence yet.

I asked her again as she was leaving, "How are you here?" "Have you come to take admission?"

The woman next to her said, "Your new literature lecturer." I'm going back slowly in bliss, knowing that I am going to see her every day, but she is straight. Does marriage make a girl in such a way that she does not even want to talk to any boy?

"Hey, my innocent bird, you haven't heard or you don't want to listen and understand that she is married, you fool." Chetan stammers as it is nearly midnight and we're drinking by sitting on the bonnet of the car.

"I heard that, and I also understood but," I said.

"But what, huh?"

As I am answering, "That asshole her husband ain't keeping her happy."

He said, grabbing my collar and shaking it vigorously, "How come you are sure about that?" "Asshole." I am explaining to him, "She said, I have a child and I am married."

"So?"

I put my arm around his neck and said, "Hey my Lallu ram! If she was happy with the marriage, she would have said first that I am married and have a child, and she said my child, not our child. Got it?"

Chetan immediately turns back and starts saying, "Swami, where are your feet?" "How do you understand all this?"

"Hey! This is the difference between you, a mortal and a great scholar like me."

We started drinking again, rattling the bottles of liquor. Looking up at the stars, I repeat her name again. "Panchi! Panchi! Oh, my Panchi! Fly me with you and take me somewhere far away in the mountains, just you and me."

Chetan,"Brother! Oh brother! "Have you fallen in love?"

"Do you know? because I don't understand anything. This time it is not feeling like you just get ultimate happiness. It is not longed for. Something else is needed. What? I don't know."

"Let's search it on Google; is it a disease or something?" Chetan started looking at something on his phone. And my eyes are fixed on the stars again," Panchi! Oh Panchi!, let's go somewhere far away."

Yawning Chetan is going from his room to the kitchen. He drinks the water and is coming toward me. I am watching all this while lying in bed. My head is hurting; everything is blurry, but not for long, as I suddenly remember, "Shit, it's 10 o'clock." "Dog, why didn't you pick me up?"

"What happened? Let's leave it today." Chetan is speaking as if he does not remember anything.

"Hey, today is Panchi's first day as our lecturer. How can we miss that?"

"Not us, just you," he said.

I asked in amazement, "So won't you come with me?"

"Any doubts?"

I challenged him, "Alright! My time will also come."

I got ready after taking a quick bath, and while taking it, I kicked Chetan and ran away.

"Where are you, the peace of my heart?" "Where are you?" Staying at one place, "Where are you?"

I asked a boy passing by, "Have you seen the new English lecturer who has come?"

"The one with cat eyes?" "Who doesn't talk and is very shy?" He said.

Oh wow! What has been told about her, but all this matches exactly with Panchi's appearance?

"Yeaah! exactly."

He pointed to the library and said, "I just saw her there."

Thanking him, I ran to the library.

And here it is. A little bird in a big library being surprised to see books that were twice as heavy as herself. As far as I think, she would be interested in stories like hers, like The Power of Being Sexy as she indeed is. Seeing her, it is understood that the girl who wears a lot of make-up along with tight, skinny clothes and thinks that she is hot is completely wrong.

"Hello mam." After hearing this, she placed the book on the shelf again and started reaching for another section. "Hey, listen to me, at least once." I folded my hands in front of her, but she was too insolent to leave again. I grabbed her by her waist and put her against the shelf. "Are you not understanding that I want to talk to you?" Now I see that I scared her and half the library too. because everyone is just looking at us. "Shall we sit and talk somewhere?" But she again nodded and said, "I am married," and was about to complete it when I stopped her midway. "I am not asking you to get married; I just want to talk to you."

"I am your teacher, and you should not talk to me about anything other than your studies."

"Thankfully, you are more than just talking about your marriage." I said with laughter, and she is leaving again.

I think I will have to take my next birth to make her mine.

"Today, I will leave only after talking to her." Everyone else started laughing when I said this. And by most, I mean Chetan, Diksha, and the two with whom we have become very good friends, Shaunak and Jasmine. Shaunak is the son of the deputy here, and Jasmine's mother teaches Hindi at this college. Despite being rich, all three of them are very down-to-earth people like us.

"Hey, it's been 3 days since you are running after her." "Has anything happened so far that will happen today?" Diksha said. "It is better that you accept my offer." "Now that too is available for free."

"Don't doubt my brother's ability, right, bro?"

"Absolutely right." I replied when Chetan said this with my support.

Shaunak also sat on the chair and said, "Let's see," and Jasmine was laughing.

Now we are watching. With long hair, kajal in the eyes, and a small black dot on the forehead, Panchi walks in a yellow and pink suit. Chal Guru Hoja Shuru, and now not only all four, but also the eyes of all the students while walking are also toward me. Now half of the college has got to know that I am dying to talk to this girl despite herself. When I am going towards her, everyone is wishing me good luck with gestures.

Chetan's voice came: "Break her leg, brother." Jasmine slaps him on the head, "It's break a leg, you idiot."

Chapter Thirteen

Panchi

Now that my husband has given me permission for a job, then this boy, yes, the same boy who looks at me wholeheartedly and then does something in such a way that everyone's attention goes towards both of us, Ugh! I hate when he does that. It is as difficult to cut his chase short as it is to understand that I am free without needing anyone's permission to do something that I want. Why is it so difficult to explain something to boys?

He doesn't understand what it means to be married. In such a situation, it is okay to think about what my aunt used to say to me so that I keep myself away from any boy.

Well, how did I get permission to do a job? Pratik is my Savior. He took out the camera footage and sent it to my husband, where Sanket was harassing me with his friends. Now I am indebted to him. When I went to his house to say thank you, he was not there. But I know that he must have gone somewhere intentionally; he does not like to take credit for whatever good he does.

Harsangeet has also started going to school. I prepare and send her to school, and at the same time I leave for college. While leaving, I worry every day that I may not meet that boy again today. which always happens, but I also do not talk to him. But today he is coming straight to me, and I see that everyone's eyes are on both of us, like every other day. He is coming near me and started saying, "The four students sitting behind me that you are seeing, I am pranking them that today you will definitely talk to me, and others are also thinking the same." "I will fall at your feet, not here but far away in the class. Just keep my shame today." And when I saw it was true, I'm not even that cruel, by the way. I told him, "Alright." And then I left smiling. This time again, there was very little talk, but I smiled, and that was something new. He slowly lifted his face toward the sky and started laughing. Everyone around him started shouting enthusiastically and started congratulating him as if he has done some great work.

The next day, when I was teaching in the class, suddenly Chetan came in panting and said, "You have been called urgently; there is a meeting; the rest can go; the lecture is over."

Everyone got up at the same time and started going out. "Hey, everyone, wait," but no one is listening. I came out, and someone grabbed my wrist and dragged me to a class. I was quite sure that it would be none other than Kabil.

"Hello, Panchi mam." As he usually says. "Let's go."

"Wait, where? "

"You will know soon," he said.

We are moving out of college. He has still grabbed my wrist and opened the car window for me. I am standing outside and he said, "Please sit, madam." "I am not kidnapping you; I know that you have a child and that you are married." I laughed at his words.

This is the first time that I am sitting in a Jeep, but I have to admit it is quite comfortable. A lot of roundabouts have passed, and I'm looking at his face; he didn't look at me even once. But why am I thinking that he should look at me?

"Did you say something?" He asked, leaning towards me.

"No". I replied.

"Let's go." He told me while opening the window on my side. He took me down by holding my hand, and it is amazing. I am not even taking my hand away from him, nor am I refusing to go with him. What is happening with me as he takes me to a green place? Such a beautiful place, which I am probably seeing for the first time in this city. "Hey, wait, what is this?" This is the Rose Garden where only lovers and couples come. And this place is full of these people only.

"Come on, thank God, your husband has brought you here at least." He laughed after saying this.

Remembering that he has never brought me here but I heard about this place. But Kabil is not taking me somewhere in the corner like other couples; he's taking me somewhere ahead. After going a little closer, I saw that there are thousands of different plants and many birds in cages. Cage is a word that somehow relates to my own world. Kabil now loosens my hand a bit and lets me roam there. I am surprised to see those birds and flowers, whereas he is to me.

"What a nice place, but why are these birds locked in cages?"

"You can free them if you want." He offered.

"Really." When I opened the first cage, the bird did not fly; after opening the second, it also did not fly. Slowly, the same thing was happening even after opening everyone else's. Seeing this, I got very upset and asked Kabil, "Why are they not flying?"

He came closer and said, "Maybe they are afraid of being free just like you."

This time something got stuck in my throat, which stopped everything—my voice and even my breathing.

"Why is it, Panchi, that you are afraid of everything? Talking, laughing out loud, making relationships" and he came closer and removed a strand of hair from my face and said, "Love."

Now, he has kissed me, and yes, I am kissing him back. There is something in him that is different from the rest. It seems like I knew what I wanted was in no one else but him. The day when I first saw him. The day we met again and this day. What is it that I kept running away from? It's running after me now. Despite being so confined, it found a way to reach me. Now we are sitting in the car again. The birds did not fly, but my dreams got freedom. Now I am becoming something more than just a married girl, and surprisingly, it is all happening on my own terms, which is love for somebody. We have stopped a bit behind on the way to my house. As we were here, he, after looking at me, opened the window at my side and helped me get down from his Jeep. We are both looking at each other as if we both have something to say; there is something that is going on in both of our minds but is finding no way to be put into words. What is this feeling that I am not afraid of anyone seeing us both standing here looking at each other in the middle of the street? But instead, I want to get even the least amount of time that I can to be with him.

Chapter Fourteen

Kabil

I don't know how my life is related to Panchi, nor do I know if I will be able to think well about this relationship in the future. But I am definitely aware that Panchi is living in a cage, and there's just so much for her to see and do. I don't want to bring any chaos into her life; I just want her to see the world outside her cage once in her lifetime. My phone rings, and I see that Jasmine has something important to tell me. When I reached there, I saw that Shaunak, Diksha, and Jasmine herself were sitting very tense, except for Chetan.

"Has anyone died?" I jokingly asked.

No one replied. "Who is it who has died?"

Then Diksha got up and said, "Our favorite lovers have come to know about them at their homes."

"Whom are you talking about?" "What do you mean?"

"The two who are sitting in front of you," Chetan said, laughing loudly. I could see that he was in control of his laughter.

Shaunak felt bad and said, "What's so funny?"

Chetan said to him as an apology, "Sorry, friend, don't be angry. I am just taking it funnily because you both knew from the very beginning that you both have different family backgrounds. Shaunak is a Pandit, whereas Jasmine is a distinct Punjabi. Why did you both go into a serious relationship? When you both know the odds."

"Exactly," Diksha said in his support.

Jaismine started crying, "What do I do now?" "My parents are now trying to get me married to some guy in Canada, and I don't want to marry him." Hugging Shaunak, she said, "I love you." "I can't be someone else's bride."

"It's ok, we are gonna find a way." Shaunak kissed her on the forehead.

After giving us a look, they both started to leave.

I tried to convince them, "Hey, stop! "If you really love each other, let's get both of you married."

Diksha stood up excitedly and said, "What! Are you serious?"

"Yes, I am."

Jaismine had her concerns about family, but the man of her life convinced her that everything would be alright when her parents will see her happy.

They have a deep chemistry that anyone can see. So, why can't their parents?

Anyways, I grabbed the keys, and everyone left downstairs except Diksha when I felt a fast heart rate and shortness of breath. It was so intense that I was barely able to move, like something was pumping out blood and stopping the heartbeat in my body to end my life. I forbade Diksha to mention this to anyone else. She told the rest to go to the Gurudwara soon, and she took me to the hospital. Now, she is waiting for me outside, and the doctor is diagnosing my illness. After measuring the electrical activity, rate, and regularity of my heartbeat using ultrasound (a special sound wave) to create a picture of the heart, he concluded that it is a coronary artery disease in which the coronary arteries struggle to supply the heart with enough blood, oxygen, and nutrients. Cholesterol deposits, or plaques, are almost always to blame. These buildups narrow your arteries, decreasing blood flow to your heart. This can cause chest pain, shortness of breath, or even a heart attack. I feel that I may not die from this disease, but its long name and knowing what it can do will definitely kill me.

"What was it?" Diksha asked me when I came out. "Nothing," I said, "just a stretch in muscles may be due to stress."

"Really! "Does it happen?" She asked in surprise.

And we also started leaving for the Gurudwara; only then did I see whom I always need to see. And how can I say this about anyone other than my Panchi? But why is she in the hospital? Coming in normal clothes, Panchi is the prettiest among all those girls who don't step out of the house without wearing Tommy or Armani. There is an elderly woman with her, whom she has caught with both hands, and an almost 18-year-old boy who sometimes looks towards Panchi by saving his eyes. The way he looks at her, he doesn't seem to be her brother. She is like this—the one who makes everyone crazy. She was about to pass me when I stopped her. Now, I did not think that she was married, and I should not stop her like this in front of everyone. It is such that now there is no idea of life, so I do not want to have any regrets while dying. She stopped, and with a twinkle in her eye, she gestured for the boy to leave. While leaving, he looked as if someone was giving a warning. I like him; he is no harm to you, Panchi.

"Mommy" screaming and laughing, a little girl is calling for her. After reaching for her, Panchi took her up in her arms. The way she looks exactly like her makes it very obvious that she is Panchi's daughter with same big round eyes, little nose, and round lips. Even though their complexions are very similar to each other, I remember that I saw her the first time I saw Panchi, but that time I didn't get a clear glimpse of her. "How come you are here?" and she said, "Ah, they are our neighbors, and it's Sunday, so I was free at home.

That's why I thought I could accompany my aunt for her physiotherapy."

"And you?" She asked me.

What should I say to her now?

"He suddenly had trouble breathing and fell to the ground. So, that's why we came to the heart doctor." Hey, this big, fat stomach could not digest such a small thing.

"What? You told me not to tell people like Chetan, but this is our English lecturer."

I slapped my hand on my forehead and pretended to be in the sun. Panchi didn't say anything; she just held my hand and kept looking at it. Tears were about to come out of her eyes. "Come on, mom, it is very sunny ." Her daughter said, I saw her concern, and to ease her tension, I said, "I am alright. It was just because of the stress. It's also in the report." Why did I have to say that "it's also in the report"? Am I trying to convince her of something that needs proof with it? She looked into my eyes and said, "I am always here, where you want someone to always be there for you." Then she left. Can I understand from this gesture of her that she loves me just because I want to? I can't even remember how many girls I've been with, but it was so easy to understand what any one of them wanted to say or wanted me to do. But Panchi is the hardest of them all. She doesn't want herself to be easier for anyone or for herself either. "Hey Panchi. Stop!" She is there looking at me and may be thinking, "What the hell he has now to make my life turn upside down?" "Let's go." To her extreme surprise, she said, "What? Where?" "There is something for you to see!" I said to her. "Hey, fatso, get to the backseat." Concerned that I may only have a few days to bring happiness into her life, now I am going to do everything fast. Diksha went to the backseat. I grabbed Panchi's wrist, looked at her, smiled, and took her to my car. "Whatever you are thinking, it's not right." She said. "Me and you." She nods her head after saying this. "Boundaries don't matter when your intentions are pure." I wanted her to believe that. The little Panchi was excited, though. She was looking at me and laughing when I saw her. Panchi didn't ask where we were going. I know she must still be thinking something very negative. When we reached the Gurudwara, everyone was waiting for us. "What's all this?" Panchi asked. I said, "This is the wedding, and we are the baraati." Harsangeet asked her to cover her head. I took a head cover from the basket and did it. I took both of their shoes by kneeling down and got these along with mine before entering the Charan Kund. The feeling was like I was with my family. I can assume whatever I want since the few days that I have left in my life are allowing me to do everything. After both Shaunak and Jasmine are tied in a knot, I have my own plans to spend the day with Panchi and her daughter, but I know Panchi. So, as per my perception of her, "There are thousands of other girls in the city; why do you want to go on some kind of date with a mother and her daughter? You need to be ashamed. We are not in America. This is India," she said. "What if we had met earlier when you were not married?" "Would you be willing to marry me?" I asked her. She said, rubbing her head and looking at her daughter, "Why does it matter now?" "It does," I said. "Everything related to you matters to me." So, tell me. "Would you have married me instead?" She is silent. "If I say I want to marry you now and be the father of your daughter, what would you say?"

Chapter Fifteen

Panchi

I really love when he grabs my hand in public. This time he said, "Did anyone tell you that your hands are like a child's?" "Soft and bumpy." I remember once when my mother placed my hands on her cheeks and said, "Look at your hands." "Even after working so much at your in-laws' house, these are still so soft." And now we are both standing in the middle of the Gurudwara, looking at each other. I am trying to fight for some words to say "yes." That yes, I will marry you. I want to marry you. But instead, I said, "We will be good friends." "Even if you get married somewhere else, we will always be friends." I have to say something, knowing that it can't be. Not that he is never going to be married, but it's me who can't be friends with him. I'm thinking about my husband, who, after knowing this, will break my legs and cut me into little pieces. I don't know what is with him—why is he running behind a girl like me, whom his family is never going to accept? "Alright! Let's keep it to friendship until now." He said.

"What do you mean by now?"

He asked, "So, will you marry me today?"

"No," I said, smiling. "That's why I said for now." He explained. He left us both at home. I mean a street behind our home. The next day, when I reached college, I saw that everyone was talking about going somewhere. From the rest of the teachers, we learned that a 5-day trip is going to Shimla, Missouri, and Nainital. Chetan and Diksha are also ready to go, except for Jasmine and Shaunak, who are both on their honeymoon in London. Kabil didn't come to college today. Chetan said that he has gone to meet his parents since last night and will come by this evening. Now that he is not there, I can ask Diksha about the incident that day. I called her in private, and she told me how Kabil did not want to let any of his friends know about this incident. If it was just because of stress, then why would he hide it from everyone? After finishing college, I went to the same hospital, and there was only one heart doctor. When I went in, I could see the doctor sitting down to examine me, due to an appointment that I had taken. "Ah, well, I am not here for a check-up," I told him. He asked curiously, "Then what?" I told him, "I am a concerned teacher. My student's name is Kabil. I wanted to know what exactly was going on with him. He is acting differently. Is he alright?"

He answered, "I can't tell you that, ma'am." "I am sorry, but it's confidential."

"That is why I am here. I am also doing my job the same as you, and I need to know. Please tell me, doctor." Then, after taking a deep breath, he told me everything about his condition. I asked, keeping my emotions under control, "How much time does he have?" "That depends." The doctor said, "I can't say much about that and can't answer you about anything else." "I understand. Well, thank you," I said when I was leaving the office. As soon as I came out, I saw Kabil standing in front of me. Nothing else was on my mind but him and the fear of how I might lose him forever. Now that everything is clear to me, why is he openly placing his feelings in front of me? I want to run and hug him and tell him everything he wants to hear. But suddenly, a voice reminded me of someone: Arnav Singh, my husband asking from behind, "What are you doing here?" I don't understand what to say. Should I tell the truth, or should I go with him in his fear as before? "What are you doing here without asking anyone one?" He asked holding my wrist very tightly. This time, when my eyes fell on Kabil, he is coming towards us very angrily and fast. I don't want to let the same thing happen here again, which happened when I met him for the first time. That's why I reached the lift with my husband even before he came near him. The lift is closing, and Kabil is looking at me amidst so many people, and I, as always, am looking at him. "How are you related to that boy?" My husband asked again in the same tone he used when he beat me the last time. But like last time, I was not so confident this time. "Which boy?" I stammered a bit. He slapped me in the moving car. "You think I am crazy." "I work the whole day for you and your daughter, and you are not at all concerned." Instead, I am just crying and saying nothing in defense. How does defending make a difference? Today he will treat me like sh*t. Tomorrow again, everything will be alright, but if I speak against it, nothing will remain the same. *Everyone is in the water, with big waves. Some cross the sea by swimming, and some float. Floating, as I consider, takes time to reach the shore, but there is no competition. It is necessary to reach the destination and keep looking up at up at the sky.* However, some drown before reaching, but I will not let Kabil drown. God, if for the sake of someone's happiness, instead of fulfilling the duties of a wife, a daughter, and a mother, I just fulfil my duty, just for the sake of some time, then I don't think you will consider it that wrong, but if you do, then please let me know because I am going to do something that a married woman should not even think of. At nearly 10 o'clock, I reached Kabil's home. But when I reached it, I saw that the house was locked. I had to wait for almost 2 hours till he came back. When I saw him, a girl wearing a black dress and heels was coming with him. They are kissing each other. Hand in hand, they were saying something to each other and laughing. Now I don't want to go in front of him. But that girl saw me. "Baby, who is she?" She asked Kabil. When he came near me, he said to her, "My teacher." Keeping his hand on my cheek, he said, "I was in love with her until yesterday, and today I love you." Then he bent down towards her and started kissing her. I started crying. Taking pity on me, the girl started telling him, "Perhaps you were not the only one who fell in love."

Chapter Sixteen

Kabil

Seeing her husband, it was known what kind of person he is. Then, knowing that I am going to die anyway, what is the point of making her life miserable? It was as difficult for me as walking on a hot cobblestone not to silence the crying Panchi and to keep watching her leave like that, but I had to do it anyhow. Life is strange too. You come to know the meaning of love when it is about to end. I had seen everything in my life except the sorrow that I felt after meeting Panchi. Not because I can't get her, because even after trying so hard, I could not bring any improvement to her life. My condition is getting worse. There is also a problem with walking. When I saw Panchi in the hospital that evening, only then did I come after meeting my parents and Tuffy. Now, the doctor has told me that plaque has hardened inside the walls of my arteries, which is blocking the flow of blood to my heart. This disease is not new to me, but I should not lie; I never went for a checkup. The doctors say that something in our lineage is causing us to die young due to coronary artery disease, but I don't accept it. Even though I have seen young deaths in our family, I never associated those with this disease, or maybe I was never told so. So, now that I am waiting to die in the hospital bed, I need all those people who have been a memorable part of my life. I just wanted to see Panchi. I just wanted to tell her that whatever she saw that day was all a lie. I wanted to say that I loved only her. I fell in love only once in my life, and I fell in love only with her. I will wait to see when we will be together again. I don't know in which birth. But I will always wait for you, Panchi. Then I remembered when she said, "I am always here, where you want someone to always be there for you." At that time only, a team of doctors came to the room. I am not in a condition to ask many questions, but they told me that a healthy heart has been found for a transplant. There was going to be a 4 to 6 hours surgery for me under general anesthesia. I wanted to know who the person is, but they said that the girl doesn't want to reveal anything about her identity before surgery. "Hey wait!" My last words before anesthesia were that I didn't want it to be the same girl whose name was in my mind. It is strange; I am going to avoid death, yet I am not happy! When I open my eyes, I see Chetan, my parents, Shaunak, Jasmine, and Diksha. I still have a breathing tube in my mouth, which is why I can't talk, but the doctors said that I am going to be able to within a 24-hour period. Right now, I am not even paying attention to anything more, maybe because of the medicines. It seems as if the heart has been found, but life is still stuck in someone. I am looking at everyone and hoping that someone will just tell me that Panchi is here, sitting outside, longing to meet me. At the same time Chetan came to me, you may have escaped from the cell only for the bird. It didn't take me long to understand that he was talking about her. Days passed. I used to wait for her, but she did not come. "Where are you?" Sometimes I ask myself, "3 months have come and gone, and you didn't have any desire to see me?" I would ask every doctor or person who come by about you. Now everyone is getting to know you here. But you didn't come. Now that I am able to walk, I can see that all that I used to hear or smell no longer exists. Doors sliding open and shut, furnaces, air exchangers, screams, cries, moans, gasps, grunts, or hisses of pain, people talking in low voices, intercoms calling out codes or directions, squeaky wheelchairs, and the scent of get-well flowers are all questionable.

Food smells from room trays: grease, meaty, soup smells. People get tired here neither from accidents or diseases nor even from death. In this hospital and the crowd of people, I also found some good friends. A surgeon who comes to check on me three times a day, whose name is Gurpreet Singh Kahlon, had an MBBS in 2014 from Punjabi University, Patiala. Then he served at PGI for four years, and now he is here, hired by Fortis in Chandigarh. He is fine in appearance, but he has money to get him a good wife. After that, an old employee, who didn't marry anyone else after his girlfriend got married, True lovers, we can say. Then comes that 14-year-old girl, whose smile is probably the cutest in the world, but the only thing is that she has a hole in her heart. She is very happy all day long, and whenever the reason for her happiness is confirmed, she has only one answer: "I am happy that I have got one more day to live."

It tells me how lucky I am to get another chance to live. I pray for the baby girl named Pawan. God blesses the innocent. This shooting bird's life is not in my hands, but yours is, Panchi.

Chapter Seventeen

Panchi

From Zirakpur, it took me about 3 hours to walk to the city. I was only thinking about Kabil while coming back. I was just crying, and nothing could understand why.

Neither he cheated on me nor did he make big promises that he could not fulfill. The only thing was that I had also fallen in love, and probably because of this, I cried seeing that girl with him. But I have to understand this thing slowly so that I can never run away from my life and my responsibilities. *You know, living in a place where you lose all sense of laughing and crying makes your life more difficult to live; it locks you in a compartment where there is neither light nor anyone who can hear your screams just like my mother.* Seeing me adopt such a life, maybe she would be very proud. Now I have become like that, as all the women in my family wanted. When I came home in the fall, I saw that my husband and all the other family members were waiting for me. It is almost 1:30 at night. All was going on in front of me like a movie, which was about to happen to me.

"Where were you till this night?" My mother-in-law asked me.

I didn't say anything and started climbing the stairs. There was nothing to say. Now it was just the power of my husband that was going to walk on me.

He came in front of me at once because, being tired, I was walking pretty slowly.

"Didn't you hear what my mother asked?" Arnav asked me very angrily.

I said, "Do you know since when I have stopped listening to any of you?" Looking at all three of them, "Now, in this house, I can only hear the words of one person, and that is Harsangeet. I hear orders from my mother-in-law. What an expense has been incurred by your father! And what a great favor you have done me by marrying me—from you. But no one wants to listen to the real thing. Even today, you are not going to communicate with me. You are just here, standing in front of me, to show your power that man gets as a blessing, dominance."

"Shameless woman, I don't know where you have come from tonight, and secondly, you are picking out faults in us." Holding my mouth tightly, he said, "You should be indebted to all of us."

I was just waiting for him to slap me and leave. But instead of that, he dragged me to the room and said,

"Your daughter will also be like you." "But if she sees what condition I am giving you today, then she will never try to do such a thing."Then it was as if my breath got stuck. He wants to show all this to a 5-year-old innocent girl. Will she also become like me? A shy girl who keeps her distance from all the boys. When she sees that she has to be confined in a box, will she also remain worried like me about whether she will be allowed to go ahead or not? He started calling Harsangeet loudly. She was looking at me and rubbing her eyes. I was more like a helpless woman with no one at her side. Just like I used to see my mother. Now my husband slapped me and dropped me on the floor. Harsangeet was coming towards me, calling out to me, falling from bed, and crying. My civil engineer husband, Mr. Arnav Singh, felt it was right to push his little daughter back. His parents were watching their son doing all this. But none of them came to save me, neither me nor their 5-year-old granddaughter. *Humanity is falling so far, I was seeing it for the first time, or was seeing it for the first time in a mother's way.* He took out his belt and started hitting me. He kept hitting me, Harsangeet kept crying, and I just kept waiting for his anger to cool down. Around 3 in the morning, he probably got tired of hitting and threw his belt down, after which he went to sleep on the sofa in our living room. I didn't dare get up and walk, but I wanted to take my daughter in my arms, hug her tightly, and tell her that everything is alright. She fell asleep on the ground. When I picked her up, she was sobbing even in her sleep. Now whatever was in front of me was the feeling of being the mother of this child, whose whole life depends on only one decision of mine. But before doing anything, it is necessary to talk to the mother once—not that I have to cry about whatever happened from beginning to end, but there is something important that should be known about being a woman. She picked up the phone and asked, "How are you, child? Is everyone okay at home? It's been so many days; there was no phone call, neither yours nor my son-in-law's."

Controlling my emotions, I said, "Mother, it is time to get out of the box. I think I am tired now. Don't you think so?"

There was no further reply. Maybe she has understood. I hung up. Due to hitting with the belt, my clothes were torn, and the color of my body turned red. I could not even walk properly. I was walking very comfortably; how would I have allowed my little Harsangeet to fall?

When I opened the door, Arnav, who was lying on the sofa, opened his eyes and was just looking at me as if he had never seen me before. Perhaps he did not think that his minor beating would make me suffer so badly. The poor guy got scared, I guess! "God bless you." Those were my last three words to him as I was leaving. I don't know why I was going towards the road. I had no phone, no money, and no place to go.

But still, I was going toward the road. While walking, I saw Gitika in sportswear; she was probably coming from jogging. She called my name loudly, and on coming running to me, she caught Harsangeet out of my arms because I was about to faint. When I opened my eyes in the morning, I saw that there was a needle in my arm and that something was being given to me through a drip. Only then did the sound of Harsangeet's screams come. I forcefully pulled the needle from my wrist and ran towards the door. When I fell again, Pratik picked me up and made me lie on the sofa, where Harsangeet was playing with Saumya. "I want to go somewhere far," I said.

Saumya, Pratik, and Gitika were all looking at me.

"Where would you go?" Saumya asked.

"Well! I guess I have a place in my mind." This thought left me with a little smile on my face.

But before leaving, I had something to do. For a few days, I was searching for those people who had good heart conditions and wanted to donate their hearts, and my search ended when I found a girl. She had an accident back in December 2012, and since then she had been crippled. Her parents support her decision. I even asked her to give her life another chance, but why is this so difficult for her? She can't even think of living right now. "I don't want to continue living, and it is better to donate your working body parts to save the lives of those who need them instead of committing suicide." I wonder what happened to her. When I visited her, there was a small house. An old woman was lying in bed coughing with three daughters surrounding her, one of whom wanted to donate her heart. She told me that her father's earnings couldn't support two patients at the same time. So, if she will take this step, they can get enough money to spend on her mother's treatment and to marry her younger sisters. The other two girls sitting on the bare ground were crying with her. I was always right; *it's not only me who has problems with her life, but everyone is doing the same in their ways. Some swim and reach the shore, but others consider floating and keep looking at the sky.*

It's been 2 months, and I have already filed for divorce. My lawyer says that there will be no problem asking for my daughter's custody since everyone can see what Arnav has done to me. I don't want his money. I think that now that I have faith in myself, I am able to give my daughter a better life.

Chapter Eighteen

Kabil

It's been 4 months, and now my condition has improved to a great extent. I am saying goodbye to all the relationships made in these 4 months, as well as to Pawan. She will have surgery tomorrow, and I will try my best to be here to see her.

"See you tomorrow, Birdie." I kissed her forehead when she hugged me. I got a little emotional, I have to say. Chetan is keeping my luggage in the car. The old employee told me while leaving, "We all will wait for you to bring Panchi here even for just once."

The cardiologist, Gurpreet Singh, said while observing his patient, "Don't you forget that." Now if I ask everyone about your arrival every day, then everyone will know about it, won't they?

I nodded my head in a hopeful yes. God knows whether you are fine or not, Panchi. My parents are also going to stay with me in Chandigarh for some days. But now that I have left the hospital, I can't think of anything else except that I want to meet you.

I told Chetan, "Just take me to Panchi's home."

"Hey, have you gone mad? What would you say if you went there? Hey, I love your daughter-in-law, and I want to meet her!"

I said, "That's the point." "How do I go?" He could see the tension, and I know he doesn't want me to stress out just after getting leave from the hospital bed.

"Calm down. I will think of something." He said.

We are watching everyone coming and going after sitting in the car for hours. "She is not going to come out of the house. Let's go." But how to convince this heart? The girl on whom he is insisting doesn't care about it at all. You haven't come to see me even once in all these months, Panchi. You didn't even try to know whether I was alive or dead. Nodding yes to Chetan, I said, "Let's go." But at the same time, "Hey! "Stop stop, stop."

"Where is Panchi?" "Where is she?" Chetan asked me.

I said, "She is not here, but someone has been found who can tell."

"Hey wait!" I called the boy with curly hair who had come to the hospital that day with Panchi.

As soon as I went near him, he took my name and said, "I was going to come to you only."

He handed me a letter and said, "Panchi had asked to give it to you."

"Where is she?" I asked him, but he said that he couldn't tell me that. I took that letter and sat on a long wooden chair at a distance.

Hi Kabil,

I don't know why, but I was always sure that you would definitely come looking for me, and here you are. I always knew that the one thing I have been craving for a lifetime is love, and God can never take that away from me. It's like something between me and him, you know. Do you know, you always used to say why I am so scared of everything, whether it is talking, laughing, or loving? I didn't know why, but now I know because of where I am standing that if there is no fear of losing something, then we don't even want to get it. Perhaps if you had not taught me to laugh, if I had not fallen in love with you, I would never have been able to take the step that I took that night. I felt very sad when I saw you with that girl. For some days, I kept thinking that you didn't love me at all, but then I slowly understood that it was only your love. Even without wanting to, you were pretending to be very happy with that girl, but your eyes, when they see me, they only see me Kabil. You could not make your eyes lie. Your eyes love me, and so do you. You love me, Kabil, and you can never deny this. Now that you and I have both got another chance to live a life, I think it would be unjust to you if I did not use it wisely and to the girl who saved your life by giving you her heart. You have given me something that I am going to carry for a lifetime—the feeling of being loved. Your love has given me the courage to get out of the box and start something new. I have always believed in destiny. I was destined to be married to Arnav, I was destined to bear a child by him, I was destined to meet you, and I know that my Destination is You only. I will reach out to you when the time is right and under the right circumstances. When there will be no one to separate us, not this society and not this traditional Panchi living inside me, Thank you for helping me out, Kabil.

I am here where you want someone to be always there for you.

Panchi.

The whole night was sleepless. I was wondering whether I should be happy to know that she is fine and away from her toxic relationships or sad that I have to wait for the miracle to see her again. While I was gone, Panchi did me a great favor; she saved my life. Perhaps I should not lose this chance given to me to live as she said. I fell in love for the first time, and it happened in a way that would never happen again. *Unknowing of the fact that love has nothing to do with physical satisfaction, I was running behind bodies but now you have told me that I was wrong. I am always yours, Panchi, and I will wait for you, until my last breath and when we meet, will you take me to the mountains with you?*